The Shark Bites Back

Pigs CAN fly!

Kweeeeeeeeeeeeeeeeeeeeeeeep!

When the Alarm Squeal sounds it must
be a job for Captain Peter Porker and
the PIGS IN PLANES!

Paul Cooper is from Manchester.
He now lives in Cambridge with
his wife and two daughters.

Read these high-flying adventures
about the Pigs in Planes:

The Shark Bites Back

PAUL COOPER

Illustrated by Trevor Dunton

PUFFIN

PUFFIN BOOKS

Published by the Penguin Group

Penguin Books Ltd, 80 Strand, London WC2R 0RL, England

Penguin Group (USA) Inc., 375 Hudson Street, New York, New York 10014, USA

Penguin Group (Canada), 90 Eglinton Avenue East, Suite 700, Toronto, Ontario, Canada M4P 2Y3
(a division of Pearson Penguin Canada Inc.)

Penguin Ireland, 25 St Stephen's Green, Dublin 2, Ireland (a division of Penguin Books Ltd)

Penguin Group (Australia), 250 Camberwell Road, Camberwell, Victoria 3124, Australia
(a division of Pearson Australia Group Pty Ltd)

Penguin Books India Pvt Ltd, 11 Community Centre, Panchsheel Park, New Delhi – 110 017, India

Penguin Group (NZ), 67 Apollo Drive, Rosedale, North Shore 0632, New Zealand
(a division of Pearson New Zealand Ltd)

Penguin Books (South Africa) (Pty) Ltd, 24 Sturdee Avenue, Rosebank, Johannesburg 2196, South Africa

Penguin Books Ltd, Registered Offices: 80 Strand, London WC2R 0RL, England

puffinbooks.com

First published 2010
3

Text copyright © Paul Cooper, 2010
Illustrations copyright © Trevor Dunton, 2010
All rights reserved

The moral right of the author and illustrator has been asserted

Set in Bembo Infant
Made and printed in England by Clays Ltd, St Ives plc

British Library Cataloguing in Publication Data
A CIP catalogue record for this book is available from the British Library

ISBN: 978–0–141–32841–6

www.greenpenguin.co.uk

Mixed Sources
Product group from well-managed
forests and other controlled sources
www.fsc.org Cert no. SA-COC-1592
© 1996 Forest Stewardship Council

Penguin Books is committed to a sustainable future
for our business, our readers and our planet.
The book in your hands is made from paper
certified by the Forest Stewardship Council.

For Bionic Beth

MEET THE CREW

PEREGRINE OINKS-
GRUNTINGTON,

Wing Commander

LOLA PENN,

Radio Operator

PETER PORKER,

Captain

TAMMY SNUFFLES,

Mechanic

BRIAN TROTTER,

Medical Officer

CURLY McHOGLET,

Trainee

ANIMAL PARADISE

N
W E
S

Chicken Island

Shark Island

Sheep Island

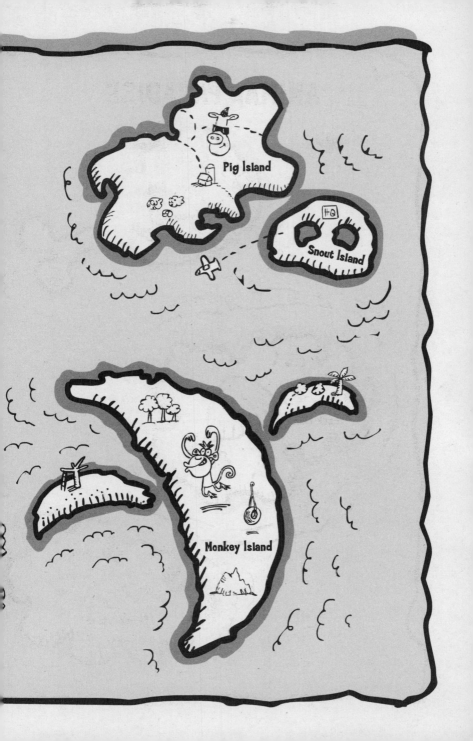

CHAPTER 1:

Fear Itself

'Have you seen Curly?' asked Captain Peter
Porker from the door of the Pigs in Planes
HQ common room. Curly was the newest
member of the PiPs team, and he was still
a trainee.

'Nope.' Tammy, the team's mechanic,
didn't lift her eyes from the TV, even though
only adverts were on.

'But –' began Pete.

Tammy shushed him. 'This is my
favourite!' she said. The advert on TV
was for a bright red fizzy drink called
SLURPO-POP. Pete noticed that Tammy

was holding a can of this drink while she watched.

In the advert, a pig with long, silky hair was saying, in the kind of voice that only people in ads ever use, '*Everything's* better with refreshingly delicious Slurpo-Pop!' She took a dainty sip, smacked her lips and went, 'Aah!'

Watching this, Tammy took a big swig, smacked her lips and went, 'BLUUUUURP!' She grinned proudly. 'It's

true – everything *is* better with Slurpo-Pop. That's the best burp I've done in months!'

Pete was about to go when he spotted something – a trail of wet footprints. They led across the room to a cupboard.

Pete followed the trail and stuck his ear to the cupboard door. 'Curly? Are you in there?'

There was a few seconds' silence, then a voice said quietly, 'Yes.'

Pete turned to Tammy. 'I thought you said you hadn't seen him.'

Tammy shrugged. 'He gave me a can of Cherry Slurpo-Pop to keep quiet, didn't he?'

Pete addressed the cupboard again. 'It's time for your advanced swimming training, Curly. There's a lot more to being in the PiPs than just flying jets.' He dropped his voice. 'What are you doing in there anyway?'

'Just . . . looking for something. Ah, here it

is! I wondered where I'd put this mop.'

The door opened a crack and Curly's usually eager young face peered out, looking much less eager than usual.

'Are you ready then?' asked Pete.

'I . . . suppose so.' Curly's eyes were wide. 'Oh, hold on! I forgot. I can't go swimming because I've got a verruca. I've got a note from my mum.'

He dug in his pocket and handed over a scrap of paper.

Pete looked at it for a moment. 'This is in your handwriting, Curly. And you've signed it *From my mum*. Come on – let's go.'

'OK,' said Curly, emerging from the cupboard, but then he added brightly: 'Wait! I haven't got my trunks today!'

'No probs. You can borrow a pair of mine.'

Curly's eyes grew even wider. Peter Porker's tiny bright red Speedio trunks *were* alarming, but that's not why Curly was panicking.

The trainee sighed. At last he said, 'The thing is . . . I'm afraid.'

'Of *swimming*?' asked Pete.

Curly shook his head. 'More of *drowning* . . . or just getting water up my snout . . . or even getting my face a bit wet, actually. I'm just afraid of water!'

'What's this? Who's afraid?' boomed a new voice from the doorway. It was Peregrine Oinks–Gruntington, the PiPs' commanding officer. 'There's no place for fear in an organization like ours!'

Curly knew this was true. The PiPs had to be ready to deal with any emergency, *anywhere* in Animal Paradise. They had to be the bravest of the brave.

Peregrine came over and put a comforting trotter on Curly's shoulder. 'I'll tell you a little secret, lad. There's only one

thing to fear in life . . . and that is *fear itself*.'

Pete thought these words of wisdom over, then said, 'What about giant robot-scorpions with lasers on their heads?'

'Or evil clowns,' Tammy chipped in. 'They'd be pretty scary.'

'Would these clowns have lasers on their heads?' asked Pete with interest.

'I think you're missing the point,' harrumphed Peregrine crossly. 'And *I'm* missing the news!' He swept up the remote control and clicked the channel over, before plonking himself firmly in the comfiest armchair in the room.

The lead story was about the camels of Camel Island complaining about the recent dry weather.

'Those camels always have the hump about something,' tutted Pete.

Then the newsreader said, 'And now over to Herbert Turbot, reporting live from Shark Island, where history is being made.'

The TV picture cut to an underwater cave where several sharks and other smaller fish were busy swimming around various bits of equipment. In the middle of them was a large hammerhead shark.

Herbert, the flatfish reporter, spoke direct to camera: 'For years, the sharks here have swum around and around their island home, never once venturing on to land, for obvious reasons. Until *today* . . . Behind me floats a hammerhead with a dream – a dream of

setting fin on dry land. Neil Headstrong
is that shark, and he is preparing today
to become the world's first ever *land shark*.
With the aid of new above-water breathing
apparatus, he will explore the island.'

Watching all this on the screen, Pete said,
'Cool!' He turned to the Wing Commander.
'Right, Peregrine?'

But the Wing Commander gave no reply.
He was frozen stiff. The only thing moving
was his huge moustache, which trembled
like a jelly in an earthquake. He tried to
speak, but the words refused to leave his
snout.

'Sh . . . sh . . . sh . . .' He lifted a shaking
trotter at the screen.

'Are you OK?' asked Curly.

'Oh, I remember now!' Tammy slapped
her forehead. 'He's got a thing about sharks.
He's absolutely terrified of them.'

She set down her drink and helped the

Wing Commander to his feet, speaking as if to a tiny piglet. 'Come on. Let's get you back to your office. No sharks in there.'

'Sh . . . sh . . . sh . . .' Peregrine allowed himself to be steered towards the door.

'We'll just watch a minute more,' said Pete. He liked to think of himself as a hero who laughed in the face of danger, and this Neil Headstrong sounded the same.

On the TV screen, Turbot was thrusting a mike towards the hammerhead. 'Neil, have you got any last . . . er, got any words for the viewers on this historic occasion?'

Headstrong nodded and grinned. 'You bet. I say . . . it's HAMMER TIME!'

From nearby came the sound of someone clearing his throat. Headstrong's grin vanished and two little lines of concentration appeared on his tool-shaped head. 'Oh, no, er . . . *One small shark steps on a kind giant . . . and leaps.*'

'Er . . . sorry, could you repeat that?' said the reporter.

'That's wrong!' said Headstrong, obviously trying to remember something. '*Step one: a small giant kinda leaps on a shark.*'

'Erm,' said Turbot, backing away carefully.

Suddenly, a smaller fish appeared from underneath the hammerhead. 'Ahem.'

'Where did he come from?' asked Curly, leaning closer to the TV. 'And why's he wearing that funny little hat?'

LIVE FROM THE SEABED

'That fish is a remora,' said Pete, 'also known as a suckerfish. And that isn't a hat on his head – it's a sucker-pad. They use them to stick themselves to the underneath of a shark and then they eat bits of leftover food.'

The suckerfish on screen smiled helpfully now at the reporter. 'If I may be of assistance . . . I think what Mr Headstrong is getting at so poetically is this – *It is one small step for a shark, one giant leap for shark-kind.*'

Headstrong nodded and grunted, 'Yeah, what he said!'

Then, with a flick of the tail, the shark put his weirdly shaped head into a big, weirdly shaped helmet full of water. A long tube connected this to a water pump. Headstrong gave a fins-up sign and swam on to a wheeled trolley. Then, using his side fins, he began to haul himself up the sloping rock of the seabed towards dry land above.

Curly settled down. He didn't care that much about the news, but as long as it kept him away from the lake, that was OK with him.

CHAPTER 2:
A Mission to Sink Your Teeth Into

The PiPs radio operator, Lola Penn, was hard at work. Ignoring the towers of paperwork on her desk, she gave her full attention to the latest copy of *Pig Puzzle Weekly!* magazine.

She read out a clue. 'Five down. "This word could be used to describe a trick." It's six letters.'

Brian Trotter, the PiPs medical officer and walking encyclopedia, was in the office writing up a report of the last PiPs mission. 'That's TRICKY,' he said.

'I know it's tricky,' said Lola. 'That's why

I'm asking you.'

Brian smiled patiently. 'You don't understand. The answer is TRICKY.'

Lola was getting cross now. 'I DO understand, thank you very much. If the answer *wasn't* tricky, I wouldn't be asking you. Now *can* you help or *can't* you?'

Brian was saved from having a pencil sharpener bounce off his head by the arrival of Tammy and the Wing Commander.

Lola watched Peregrine shuffle to the desk in his office. He slumped in his chair, still staring forward blankly and going, 'Sh . . . sh . . . sh . . .'

'What's up with him?' Lola asked.

When Tammy explained about the shark on the TV, Lola reached for the emergency pack of chocolate biscuits in her desk.

Ten minutes later, Peregrine was nibbling bicky number forty-seven. He was still staring blankly, but at least he'd stopped mumbling.

Brian and Tammy had gone, leaving Lola to work her way through the prize crossword alone. A beep from the radio interrupted her.

'Pigs in Planes,' she said into her headphone mike. 'State your island, species and the nature of the problem.'

As she listened, her expression grew more and more grave. She reached out and pressed a red button:

*KWEEEEEEEEEEEEEEEEE
EEEEEEEEEEEEEEEEEEEEE
EEEEEEEEEP!*

The Code Pink emergency
squeal rang out from
loudspeakers all over Snout
Island. Somewhere in Animal
Paradise someone was in need of
help. Someone needed the Pigs in
Planes!

Wherever they were, the PiPs
started making for the exits. Pete
and Curly legged it from the
TV room; Brian ran from the
library; Tammy trotted from the
kitchen where she'd been eating
ice cream out of the tub without
a spoon.

Once outside, they all started
running towards the jets. Lola's

voice came over the loudspeakers: 'PiPs, you'd better double up and just take SkyHogs 1 and 3.'

'Why's that?' Curly asked Pete as they ran.

'Tammy's been refitting the jets with special skis for when there's no land to touchdown on. She's only finished those two planes so far.'

Curly slowed down. 'You mean . . .?'

Pete grinned. 'Wherever we're going, we're landing on water!'

Back in the office, Lola waited for the sound of the jet engines. 'Here are your co-ordinates, PiPs.' She read out a map reference, and then glanced quickly towards the Wing Commander's office. She dropped her voice to a whisper: 'You're going to Shark Island.'

Pete's voice came back over the radio. 'What was that, Lola? I didn't catch it. There must be some interference.'

'I said, you're going to Shark Island,' repeated the radio operator in a normal voice. She looked nervously again at Peregrine's office. The Wing Commander was still staring into space. Lola didn't think he had heard her.

But Pete's voice came over the radio again. 'Nope, still didn't quite get it. One more time, please, Lola. *Where* are we going?'

'TO SHARK ISLAND!' Lola bellowed.

She saw Peregrine leap out of his chair as if he'd been electrocuted.

'Sh . . . sh . . . sh . . .' he began to mumble again, his mind filled with dark thoughts of triangular fins and jagged teeth.

As the two jets reached cruising speed, Brian, piloting SkyHog 3, heard a noise from the cockpit behind him.

'You didn't just open a can of Slurpo-Pop,

did you?' he asked over his shoulder.

'Sure did!' said Tammy. 'It's refreshingly delicious!'

Brian pointed to a sign in the cockpit:

THANK YOU FOR NOT EATING OR DRINKING.

'That doesn't mean me, does it?' asked Tammy.

Brian pointed to the bottom of the sign, which said:

THAT MEANS YOU, TAMMY.

'Oh.' The mechanic shrugged. 'May as well drink it now it's open.'

Brian tutted. 'Anyway, Slurpo-Pop contains no real fruit juice at all, just additives and chemicals.'

'I know!' agreed Tammy eagerly. 'It's additive E45625x that gives it a real kick!'

In SkyHog 1, Pete was speaking to HQ over the radio. 'What's the situation, Lola? Has it got anything to do with the world's first ever land shark? Over.'

'How did you know?' replied Lola, back at PiPs base.

'Just a lucky guess,' grinned Pete. 'Also, we saw it on telly.'

Lola filled them in: 'Headstrong was on land for fifteen minutes when they lost radio contact. There must have been some sort of accident with the line because no seawater was getting through to him! No shark can go on land to help him, so they called us. We have to rescue Headstrong and get him back into the water.'

Brian's voice came over the radio. 'According to my calculations,' he said, 'Mr Headstrong could survive for sixteen minutes and forty-two seconds on the amount of water left in his helmet.' He paused. 'Give or take a half-second.'

Pete glanced at his watch. 'That leaves about five minutes to save him! Curly and

Tammy, get ready to parachute in.'

After all the fuss about the swimming session, Curly didn't want Pete to think he was a scaredy-pig.

'You bet!' he called out. He double-checked all the straps and cords on his parachute pack. Tammy did the same in SkyHog 3.

'Now remember,' Pete told the trainee slowly and carefully. 'You have to pull the blue cord, not the red one. Got it? Blue, not red. Now, which cord are you going to pull?'

'The blue one,' said Curly.

'OK, we're almost at the island,' said Pete. 'Get ready!' He pressed a button and a hatch slid open above Curly. A second button activated the spring under Curly's seat. It boinged up and – WHOOSH! – Curly shot into the big, blue sky.

Looking down, he could see Tammy's open chute and the ground rushing towards

him. It was rocky, but that didn't bother him. What bothered him was the big lagoon of water right in the middle of the island.

WATER! That couldn't be right – he'd been looking at a map of Shark Island on the plane and it hadn't shown water inland! But there it was, twinkling in the sunshine – and he was hurtling straight towards it. Curly was so shocked he suddenly couldn't remember which cord to pull. *Red? Blue? Red? Blue?*

He pulled the red cord. Immediately, a flap in his pack opened up and two cheese-and-pickle sandwiches, an orange and a hard-boiled egg flew out.

Wrong cord!

His trotter reached for the other cord, but panic had taken hold of him now. The cord was being blown backwards by the rush of air and he couldn't get a trotter to it. He couldn't think of anything else but the water he was freefalling towards. His mind searched frantically for something appropriate to say. Finally, it settled on the old classic:

'AAAAAAARRRRGGGHHH!'

CHAPTER 3:

Hammer Time!

Back at PiPs HQ, Peregrine was on his feet.

'Do you have a minute?' he asked Lola.

She quickly slid her copy of *Pig Puzzle Weekly!* under some work documents and nodded.

'I suppose you're wondering why I react so strongly whenever I see a . . . you-know-what,' said the Wing Commander.

'Not really,' replied Lola.

'I'll tell you then . . .' Peregrine pulled up a chair in front of the radio operator's desk. 'This all happened years ago . . . before I joined the Porcine Air Force . . . before

Animal Paradise was even set up!'

Peregrine stared straight ahead, but he wasn't looking at Lola's pop posters on the wall. What he was looking at lay in the past – back in the Bad Old Days when some animals still felt it was OK to eat other animals just because they were tasty.

'I was working on a merchant ship,' continued Peregrine. 'It was my first voyage, and it turned out to be my only one. That's because we hit a reef and the ship began to sink. I found myself adrift at sea, sitting on top of a crate.' His eyes met Lola's, and she saw the look of horror in them. 'The first of the sharks arrived before dawn. I spotted their fins, cutting through the water. Soon three or four tiger sharks were circling me.'

'What did you do?'

'I fell in.'

Lola tried not to laugh. 'What then?'

'I don't know. I half-remember a huge mouth full of teeth and the hungry blackness of a shark's eye. After that, my memory is a blank,' continued Peregrine. 'The next thing I recall is sitting inside the rescue plane.'

Lola thought this over. 'If those sharks really wanted to get you, how did you manage to escape unhurt?'

'I didn't,' said Peregrine, grimly rolling up one trouser leg. 'See this scar?'

Lola studied the mark on Peregrine's calf. 'That's just cos your socks are too tight, isn't it?'

'No, not there. *There!*'

Lola looked again and finally spotted a small pale scar. 'That?' she grunted. 'You call that a scar? I've got bigger scars from when I fell over trying out my new flip-flops!'

Peregrine had a haunted look in his eyes. 'The real scars are on the inside,' he whispered.

'Sorry I clipped your parachute in mid-air,' said Curly, dusting himself off.

'That's OK,' said Tammy.

In fact, Curly had crashed into the top of Tammy's parachute canopy, tangling it up and sending her hurtling down to earth too. At the last minute, and completely by accident, Curly had pulled his blue cord. As his chute opened, a lucky gust of wind carried them past the mystery body of water. Just clearing a line of trees, they had finally landed on the ground like two sacks of spuds. All in all, it had *not* been a textbook PiPs operation.

'And sorry I landed on top of you.'

'OK.'

Curly nudged the remains of a flattened orange with the toe of his boot. 'And sorry I lost our packed lunch.'

'OK, stop saying sorry!' exclaimed Tammy. 'We've got about four minutes to find that shark before he makes like a frog and croaks!'

She consulted her compass, and the two pigs raced up one of the hills that ringed the middle of the island. When they got to the top of the ridge, they soon found what they were looking for – large, helmet-wearing sharks sprawled out on the ground were pretty easy to spot. Headstrong's tail flapped weakly in the dust. The wheeled trolley lay upside down a few metres away. One of the wheels had come off.

'Quick!' said Tammy.

Curly reached the stranded shark first.
After that embarrassing mess-up with the
parachutes, he was going to do this right.
He was going to follow the guidelines of the
PiPs Operational Manual to the letter.

'Excuse me, sir?' he said.

The hammerhead shark turned its head
feebly.

'Good morning.' Curly glanced at his
watch. 'Er, sorry, I mean, good afternoon.
My name is Curly McHoglet and I am with

the Pigs in Planes. Well, I'm only a trainee, actually, but anyway . . .'

The look of hope in the hammerhead's eye was starting to fade.

'I just need to confirm one thing. Is your name . . .' Curly looked quickly at his notepad, '. . . Neil Headstrong?'

The hammerhead could only manage a faint gasp.

'*Of course* that's Headstrong!' cried Tammy, joining them. 'How many hammerheads do you think there are strolling around up here with giant water-helmets on their bonces?'

She began to check the water supply. Maybe a rock had simply fallen on top of it? She followed the water line, but her hopes soon died. Just metres from where the shark lay, the line had been cut. There was no chance of joining the two ends with tape – they had been shredded.

'We have to get him back into the water,'

she said. 'But I don't think we've got enough time to get him back to the sea.'

'What about that lagoon in the middle of the island?' Curly piped up. 'That's much closer!'

Tammy nodded. She flipped the trolley back over and reconnected the wheel. Then together they began to haul the big shark back towards the trolley. Headstrong helped as much as he could, flapping his pectoral fins and tail, but his strength was almost gone.

Finally, with most of the shark's body back on the trolley, they managed to push it to the edge of the ridge.

'This is too slow,' said Curly, but Tammy had an idea. Once they were over the ridge, both pigs pushed the trolley downhill as fast as possible. When it had gathered enough speed, they hopped on to the trolley themselves, each holding on to the hammerhead's dorsal fin. They were going to ride that shark all the way down to the water!

Curly loved this. It was like riding the world's coolest skateboard. 'Wheee!' he cried. 'What a fantastic way to end the mission!'

'It's not over just yet, Curly,' said Tammy darkly, reaching for her radio. 'Pete, Lola, do you read me?'

'Loud and clear,' came the reply from Pete.

'We have a problem. It's Headstrong's water supply . . . It was no accident. I think somebody cut it.'

CHAPTER 4:

Something Fishy

'Are you feeling OK, Bri?' asked Pete.

The two pilots had lowered the planes'
water-skis and landed SkyHogs 1 and 3 on
the water off the west coast of Shark Island.
Now they were bobbing up and down in a
little dinghy. The swell of the sea was quite
gentle, but Brian was a shade of green that
went quite nicely with the yellow of the
inflatable boat.

'Ahem,' said a voice from behind the boat.
A fish was poking its head out of the water
and Pete recognized it. It was that little
suckerfish he had seen earlier on TV. Its grey

sucker-pad looked even yuckier out of the water.

'It's a pleasure to meet the famous Pigs in Planes,' it said. 'Quite, quite *splendid.*' His sucker-pad quivered. 'I'd be happy to help in any way I can.'

'You can start by telling us who you are,' said Pete.

'My name is Watson,' said the suckerfish. 'It has been my honour to work for Mr Headstrong for several months.' After each sentence, the fish ducked under the surface to take in water through its gills.

'Does he have any enemies?' asked Pete, getting down to business. 'Anyone who might want to *kill* him?'

The suckerfish looked shocked. 'Goodness, no! Surely today's unfortunate events were an accident.'

'Think again, sucker-boy,' said Pete. 'But don't worry – whoever tried to bump him off didn't succeed, and now the PiPs are on the case. Even as we speak, two of our finest operatives are on the island. Your hammerhead's in safe trotters.'

The suckerfish blinked. 'Oh, I see . . . *Splendid.*'

'In fact,' said Brian, 'we're waiting for them here. When we flew over the island, we saw a channel of water running down to this stretch of coast. Can you point it out for us?'

Watson gave an apologetic look. 'I'm afraid you're mistaken,' he said. 'There's no waterway into, or out of, the island here.'

'What about underwater?' asked Pete.

The suckerfish shook his head. 'I can assure you there's nothing. In fact, the sharks tend to avoid this spot. You could look for yourself, but it can be rather dangerous here. There are pockets of underwater gas under the reef.'

'We'll just wait then,' said Pete.

'*Splendid.*' Watson rubbed his front fins together. 'Then perhaps I can get you something to eat? We do a tasty kelp burger here at Shark Island. Or perhaps you'd prefer a lovely seaweedy kelp fritter?'

'No!' said Brian, a little too quickly. 'Thank you.'

'Maybe a scrummy sun-dried kelp pattie?' offered Watson.

'That's OK, thanks,' said Pete. 'But don't

worry – if we need kelp, we'll call you.'

As Watson swam away, Pete said, 'No wonder he was sucking up to us. Did you see that sucker-pad on his head?'

'At least he was helpful,' commented Brian.

Pete nodded thoughtfully. 'Seems like a bit of an oily fish, though.' He began checking his oxygen tank.

'What are you doing?' asked Brian. 'That suckerfish just said these were dangerous waters.'

Pete shrugged. 'Danger is my middle name.'

'Your middle name is *Tiberius*,' corrected Brian.

Pete swapped his shades for goggles. 'I just want to check it out for myself, Bri. I know there's a channel of water on the island because I saw it myself. I can't help thinking there's something fishy about this place.' He

gave Brian a wink
as he pulled on his
flippers. 'Get it? *Something
fishy*. You know, cos
sharks are fish?'
Brian stared
blankly. He knew
a lot about many
things, but the captain's
awful jokes were
often as murky to
him as the water Pete
now dived into with a huge *SPLASH*!

As the trolley trundled along, Tammy
and Curly could see the sparkle of water
through the trees ahead. Not far to go
now, but would they make it in time? The
hammerhead shark had begun letting out
some alarming gasping noises. His skin
looked like a gigantic prune.

At the bottom of the hill, the pigs hopped off and ran alongside the shark, pushing with all their strength. Once they cleared the trees, they saw a big lake right in the middle of the island. It was surrounded by a low concrete wall.

'But this island's supposed to be untouched!' gasped Tammy. 'How's there a wall here?'

A more pressing question was how to get a big shark over that wall. As they got closer, they realized they didn't have to. There was a large, deep pool to the side of the lagoon with no barrier around it. It was their only hope.

The pigs put on a final sprint. As they screeched to a halt at the pool's edge, the trolley stopped, but the hammerhead shark didn't. Headstrong shot straight into the pool and slammed head-first into the side. His helmet cracked in half and sank to the bottom as he drank in the lovely, oxygen-rich saltwater.

It was only then that the two pigs realized the pool wasn't empty. There were several fish swimming around in there, not to mention eels and octopi. Many of these hid in the corners when Headstrong plunged into the water.

However, a cod did stick its head out of the surface and call to the two pigs. 'OY!'

'Good afternoon!' Curly called. 'My name is –'

'No time for formal introductions!' cut in Tammy. 'What's going on here?'

'Go and get help!' the cod shouted. 'We're prisoners!'

An eel began to swim up to the surface to add something. It was still underwater so its words sounded like 'BLUBBLUBBLUBBA!'

A narrow strip divided this pool from a second, which had less water in it. The pigs ran out along this causeway now to hear the eel better. They didn't notice the pile of seaweed until Curly skidded on it. He fell backwards, grabbing Tammy to steady himself.

As both pigs tumbled back, the eel poked its head out of the water: 'What I said was, don't come any closer, or else you'll slip on the seaweed.'

But the pigs didn't hear this because by now they had fallen into the other pool.

They kerplunked into the murky water at the bottom.

As salty water shot up his snout, panic seized Curly. He began flailing around and spluttering, 'I'm drowning! Help meeeeeeee!'

'Er . . . Curly?'

'No! I'm drowning! I'm –'

Curly paused.

He looked at Tammy, who was standing up. The water came to just above her knees.

'Oh,' said Curly, getting up. 'Right.'

They looked around. This pool was the same as the other, except with much less water in it. The two pools – which were beginning to seem more like fish-tanks – were separated by a solid wall. However, the side of the tank alongside the lagoon was different. This was made of clear, thick glass, which meant they could look out into the deep, dark waters of the lagoon.

'This is so strange,' said Tammy. 'Who has

built all of this? Supposedly no one has ever come on to this mainland before. And here's another question for you – why? Why is there a big lagoon that doesn't even appear on the map of Shark Island?' She grabbed her radio to contact Lola for the answer, but as she held it up water seeped out of the sides. 'Oops.'

Curly's radio was leaking water too. 'I've got another question,' he said. He pointed at the smooth walls of the tank all around them, much too high to climb. 'If we can't call for help . . . how are we going to get out of here?'

CHAPTER 5:

Be a Chum

Pete usually loved diving. It was like flying, but with added fish and bubbles.

But today was different. Something about this whole situation here at Shark Island bothered him. As he swam, he checked the rocky coast carefully. Nothing seemed out of the ordinary, but Pete listened to his gut feelings and dived deeper, into the darker waters where the island rose from the seabed. He ran his underwater torch beam across waves of thick seaweed. Still nothing.

He was about to swim back up to the surface, when he caught a glimpse of something. Inside a crack in the rocky seabed, surrounded by seaweed, there was something colourful. Something with writing on it – a poster.

Pete was able to fit only his head and one arm into the crack, but it was enough for him to grab the tattered poster. It said:

FISH! OTHER SEA CREATURES!*

Are you looking for a new job with great benefits?
There are exciting career opportunities with
CHUM LUXURY BREAKS.
Work outdoors and stay in shape!
Get your teeth into a new way of life on Shark Island!

* Sea cucumbers need not apply.

Puzzling, thought Pete.

He was a pig of action; puzzles just gave him a headache. He needed Brian to apply his enormous brain to the problem. As he turned to go, Pete's wetsuit snagged on a rock. As he unhooked himself a giant shark emerged from the gloom, gliding like a ghost in the darkness – a three-tonne ghost with a great big mouth full of serrated choppers, that is. It was a great white shark, the most fearsome shark of all. Just the slightest flick of its mighty tail powered it forward.

Pete slunk further back into the seaweed that was hiding him.

Two more shadows appeared. These sharks were just as big, their jet-black eyes just as scary.

The *sensible* thing to do was swim up and question them. That's what the *PiPs Operational Manual* would recommend. After all, Pete had no reason to believe that they were up to no good. Why shouldn't there be sharks at Shark Island?

But Pete put more faith in his own gut instincts than the PiPs manual, and right now his gut was screaming, 'Don't go up there, boss! PLEASE!'

He crouched down in the seaweed and watched as the three sharks came to a halt above him. A little pilot fish shot ahead of them to a spot halfway up the rocky side

of the island. It nosed aside a starfish and
started prodding at a button.

Moments later, a large circular panel in
the rock slid open. A hidden entrance!

Pete guessed this must be where the
channel of water on the island joined the
sea. He watched in amazement as the three
sharks followed the pilot fish into this secret
entrance. Seconds later, the panel door slid
shut behind them.

Pete's mind was racing. Whatever was going on here, he didn't like it. He kicked up towards the surface and the waiting dinghy.

Behind him the sea floor was quiet and still . . . at first. Then something stirred. It looked as if the seabed itself was moving. In fact, it was an angel shark. Its body was as flat as if it had been run over by a steamroller. This, along with its sandy-patterned skin, allowed it to hide on the seabed. It was the perfect underwater spy. The eyes on top of its head had watched Peter Porker's every move.

Now all it had to do was go and report everything to the Big Boss.

Curly looked in alarm at the blood stain on Tammy's flightsuit. 'You hurt yourself in the fall!' he exclaimed.

'Stay calm, kid,' Tammy said, holding up a can of drink. 'That's just Cherry Slurpo-Pop.'

She belched as she studied the walls of the tank. 'I'll have us out of here in two shakes of a piglet's tail.'

As well as a multi-pack of Slurpo-Pop, Tammy's backpack also contained a trusty length of rope and a grappling hook. She never went anywhere without these – even the supermarket or disco.

Tammy whirled the hook around a few times, then threw it up to the edge of the tank. On the first go, the hook didn't catch on anything; it came crashing back down into the water. The same thing happened on the next throw.

On the third attempt, Tammy whirled the rope faster and threw the hook harder. It flew up, and over the edge. There was a distinct *CLICK!*, then the hook fell back down into the water again.

'I think it hit some kind of button!' cried Tammy.

'But what does the button do?'

Moments later they found out. There was a low electric hum as a panel halfway up the tank wall slid open. Gallons of water began to gush into the tank.

'Oops!'

Curly looked in terror at the water frothing around his legs. 'It's going to fill up!'

His worst nightmare was coming true. (Well, *second* worst – this wasn't as bad as the nightmare where he went shopping wearing only a pair of polka-dot socks.)

The water level was rising fast. It had started just above his knees. Soon it was halfway up his thighs, and climbing second by second.

'What are we going to DOOOOOO?' Curly delivered this final word in a high-pitched yowl as the chilly water reached his private bits.

Tammy was still keeping a level head.

'Don't panic!' she cried. 'As the level rises, we'll just float to the top and get out that way!'

'I don't think I CAN float!' wailed Curly. The water was at his belly button now.

'A piece of *wood* can float!' said Tammy.

But then, with another whirring noise, a second mechanism kicked into action and a clear plastic lid began to slide slowly across the top of the tank.

'Can we panic *now*?' asked Curly. The water was up to his armpits.

Tammy looped the rope and hook one last time, twirling it over her head like a lasso. She threw with all her strength.

Curly was on tippy-trotters now to keep his snout above water.

'It worked!' cried Tammy. 'It caught on something!' There was another clicking noise as the hook struck a second button. Tammy pulled the rope taut and got ready

to climb up the wall.
But as soon as she
put her weight on
it, the rope came
tumbling back
towards them once
again . . . this time
without the hook!

The lid was more
than halfway across
now. Curly didn't
think things could
get worse, but then it
became clear what
the second button
was for, as dramatic
music began to
play from a hidden
speaker. It was the
theme music from a
classic horror movie

about killer sharks from the Bad Old Days —
*Choppers II: Just When You Thought It Was Safe
to Go Back in the Paddling Pool.*

Tammy was treading water now, with one
arm round Curly's neck to keep his head
above water.

'What now?' cried Curly.

Tammy thought it over. Soon the cover
would be completely shut and not long after
that the tank would fill with water. Even the
world's most hopeful pig would struggle to
describe this as a 'glass-half-full' situation. It
was more one of those 'death-trap-almost-
completely-full' situations.

'*Now* might be the time to start
panicking,' she admitted.

So they did.

CHAPTER 6:

A Bumpy Ride

As soon as Pete was back in the dinghy, he radioed HQ. There was a crackling noise, then Lola's voice said, 'PiPs HQ here. What's going on, Pete? We haven't heard a word from Tammy and Curly.'

'Not sure,' answered Pete as he swapped his goggles for his mirror shades. 'But can you check something?' He explained about the poster he'd found underwater. To make sure Lola got the name right, Pete used the International Spelling Alphabet: 'CHUM ... That's Crisps, Hollyhocks, Underpants, Marzipan.'

'Got it,' said Lola.

'There's more –' Pete began. He was going to explain about the secret entrance and the great whites. He wanted to ask Lola to check the latest satellite photos of Shark Island for the mysterious lagoon and waterway they had spotted from above.

However, he didn't get the chance. Suddenly, the dinghy rocked wildly, and the radio slipped from Pete's trotter. It landed in the sea with a sad little PLOP!

Pete looked at the calm water around them.

'I don't think that was a wave,' said Brian. 'Something just passed under the boat!'

Pete peered over the side, expecting to see a shark. Instead he saw something much smaller swimming away – the pilot fish who'd let the Great Sharks into the island!

'Follow that fish!' cried Pete.

They started paddling furiously. The pilot

fish was fast, but the pigs kept it in their sights.

'It's heading towards the island!' shouted Brian.

They renewed their efforts, but suddenly the pilot fish shot down into deeper water. Soon after that the pigs saw the first fin break the surface. It knifed its way towards them. No longer paddling, both pigs felt a shiver of anxiety. Even in Animal Paradise, a shark's fin coming towards you was one of nature's scariest sights – right up there with finding that a gang of warthogs has gatecrashed your tea party.

A tiger shark's head reared out of the water.

'Have you seen a pilot fish pass this way?' asked Brian urgently. 'We've reason to believe it's involved in illegal activity that may have something to do with what happened to Neil Headstrong.'

The tiger shark just stared blankly. Its teeth looked sharp, and there were altogether too many of them.

'It might be heading to a secret underwater entrance into the island,' continued Pete. 'Can you help?'

The shark showed even more teeth.

'I'm not sure he understands,' said Brian. (Sharks weren't famous for their brainpower.)

Pete was sure. 'You saw that pilot fish, right?' he asked the shark.

Its black eyes glittered as it gave a little nod.

'But you're not going to help because whatever's going on, you're *IN ON IT*. Right?' the captain challenged.

The tiger shark's mouth widened into an odd, toothy grin. 'Right,' it snarled. Behind it, several other fins were heading over.

In the middle of them, the pilot fish

popped its head out. 'Got it in one, pig!' he
called. He swam closer to the boat. 'I take it
you saw the great white sharks then?'

Pete snorted. 'Let's not go over the top.
I wouldn't say *great* – they were OK.'

The shark fins had begun circling the
boat menacingly.

'What's going on inside the island?' Brian
demanded. 'Our team-mates are there and
we're worried about them.'

The pilot fish pulled a mock sad face.
'Boo hoo! Don't think you'll be seeing your

little chums again!'

'Why, what's going to happen to them?' demanded Pete.

'You should be worrying more about what's going to happen to *you*,' snapped the pilot fish. 'We can't let you share our secret with the world. Right, lads?'

Brian realized what the odd expression on the tiger shark's face was – *peckish*.

The pilot fish dived underwater and reappeared at the back of the dinghy.

'Dinnertime!' he cried. And then he sank his teeth into the back of the inflatable boat with a POP! He probably expected the dinghy to sink immediately, but his mouth wasn't wide enough. Instead air began to zoom out of the little hole, and this pushed the boat forward . . . towards the jaws of the waiting tiger shark.

'Lean right!' cried Pete.

The two pigs hurled themselves to the

side, causing the dinghy to swerve. Like an air-powered motorboat, the dinghy picked up speed as more air rushed out.

'We're on course for the plane!' cried Pete through the sea spray. He tried to ignore the fins slicing through the water behind them.

But then another shark loomed ahead.

'Left!' cried Pete.

Again they leaned just in time to avoid the shark. They were *so close* to the SkyHogs, but now they'd turned away from them. Apart from a tiny desert island jutting out of the water, nothing lay ahead but open sea.

Another fin loomed in front of them.

'Lean!' shouted Pete.

'Which way?'

'Left!'

'Sorry, was that *left*?'

'Right!'

'Is that right as in *correct* or *right as in the opposite of left*?'

Pete had no time to answer – they struck the shark head on. For a couple of seconds Pete felt himself flying through the air. Then he splashed down into the cold water. He began to piggy-paddle as fast as he could, knowing that sharks were close behind.

Suddenly he felt sand beneath his trotters. He scrambled up it on all fours. Brian was right beside him.

They were on the little desert island!

There was nothing here but one rock and a single palm tree, then sandy beach sloping down to the sea on all sides. Annoyingly, SkyHog 1 was no more than twenty-five metres away – the problem was that this was twenty-five metres of shark-infested water.

'What now?' moaned Brian. The medic was pulling the pieces of his smashed radio out of his pocket.

Pete looked towards the main island.

'We hope Tammy and Curly are getting on better than us.'

Things could hardly be worse for Tammy and Curly.

With the plastic lid completely covering the holding tank, there was no way out. They had tried pounding on the cover, but all they got was bruised knuckles. Only about a foot of airspace was left at the top of the tank, and still the water poured in.

Suddenly, they realized they were being watched. Out in the lagoon, a suckerfish was looking through the glass wall into the tank. It started opening and closing its mouth.

'What's it saying?' cried Curly. 'Can you read lips?'

'Not fish lips!' said Tammy.

The suckerfish began to do a mime with his tail and fins.

'It's acting out a message!' cried Tammy.

The pigs had to tilt their heads back and poke their snouts up to gasp in the remaining bit of air. In his panic, Curly's brain tossed up the idea that the suckerfish was playing a bizarre game of Charades.

'Is it a film?' he cried in desperation. 'How many words?'

The suckerfish continued waggling its fins.

'Is it *The Lizard of Oz*?'

'What are you going on about?' asked Tammy, still keeping a lifesaver hold on the frantic young pig.

On the other side of the glass wall, the suckerfish was ducking his head down and swimming round in tight circles.

The water inside the tank was almost at the very top. The pigs' heads were pressing against the see-through plastic lid. Unless they grew themselves gills in the next few seconds, they were goners.

Suddenly Tammy grinned. 'I get it! He's saying – *SWIM DOWN . . . AND PULL OUT . . . THE PLUG!'*

'I don't know that movie,' wailed Curly. 'Who's in it?'

'Nobody! There is no movie. There's a plug! A plug at the bottom of this tank!'

There was no time for further discussion, only enough to take one final, huge gulp of air, before the water bubbled over their heads.

Tammy let go of Curly and began to frog-kick to the bottom. The

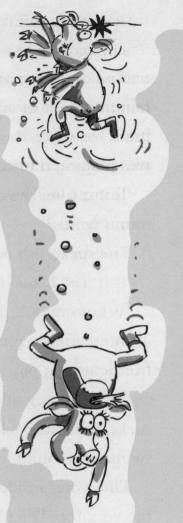

trainee began flailing about in the water. The only way she could help him now was to find that plug. Her lungs felt as if they'd burst by the time she reached the base of the tank, but there it was . . . a great, big rubber plug attached to the floor by a chain.

Tammy grabbed it and yanked.

CHAPTER 7:

Talking Food

When it came to digging up info online, Lola was an expert. Her trotters flew over the keyboard in the search for information on the job ad Pete had mentioned. The name 'CHUM Luxury Breaks' made it sound as if the company offered holidays of some kind. However, Lola could find no site for the company, and no mention of it on other sites.

'What are you doing now?' asked Peregrine, who didn't trust any technology developed after the bicycle.

'I'm checking the Animal Paradise

central government files,' said Lola. 'All new businesses have to register with them.' She scrolled down a long list of names, until: 'Here it is!'

There was no information listed for CHUM Luxury Breaks except the name of the company's owner.

'Mr A. Roe,' Lola read out. 'Funny name for a shark.'

When she did a search on this name, she came up with nothing.

'It's almost like he doesn't exist,' she said. Her eyes fell on the copy of *Pig Puzzle Weekly!* 'Hold on a moment . . .'

'Now's no time for silly puzzles!' grumbled Peregrine.

Lola ignored him. She swept up a pencil and wrote:

MR A. ROE

'If you unscramble the letters,' she said, 'you can make a new word. Look.'

She began to rewrite the same letters in a different order:

REMORA

She looked up. '*Remora?* That's another name for *suckerfish*, isn't it?'

Peregrine looked shaken. An old memory was bubbling up to the surface of his mind.

'It must mean something,' Lola was saying. 'There was a suckerfish on Headstrong's support team, wasn't there? Perhaps we should call and see if he can help?'

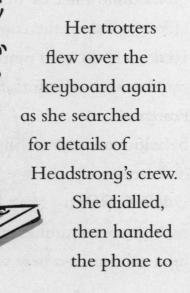

Her trotters flew over the keyboard again as she searched for details of Headstrong's crew. She dialled, then handed the phone to

Peregrine. 'Here – it'll sound better from you.'

In a daze, Peregrine took the phone. He said nothing but he listened intently. The phone fell from his trotter with a clatter.

Lola grabbed it and caught the end of the answerphone message. A polite voice was saying, 'If you wish to leave a message for Anthony Watson, please do so at the sound of the gurgle. That would be *splendid*!'

Lola put the phone down. 'Why didn't you leave a message?'

Peregrine couldn't stop trembling. 'I remember . . .' he whispered. 'I remember what happened twenty years ago!'

'What now?' asked Pete.

He and Brian could walk around the whole of their little desert island in twenty paces. The sharks continued to circle, each one seeming to occupy his own 'swimming lane' around the little island. Every so often, a sinister grey head broke the surface and smirked scarily.

Pete plonked himself down on the rock. Any plan to get off this island was more likely to spring from Brian's brain.

'I'll just sit here and work on my tan,' he said.

'What?'

'I said, I'll just sit here and work on a PLAN,' Pete replied, tilting his head back so the sun caught underneath his chins.

Meanwhile Brian was rifling through his medical kit. 'Got it!' He held up an old tube. 'I packed this,' he said. 'Just in case.'

Pete squinted at the tube in Brian's trotter. It looked very old. The lettering on the side said *Fletcher's Finest Anti-Shark Gel*.

'I found it in the supply cupboard,' explained Brian. 'It's from the Bad Old Days. I think it was Peregrine's.' He started reading the instructions on the tube. 'You have to rub it all over.'

Pete was curious. 'And does it stop sharks from eating you?'

Brian studied the small print. 'It says, "The makers cannot guarantee that no shark will consume you if you use *Fletcher's Finest Anti-Shark Gel*. However, we can guarantee that nine out of ten sharks will not enjoy eating you so much. Your money back if not completely satisfied with this product!"'

'Great!' Pete snorted. 'I'll get a refund if I end up as a pork dinner? No thanks! Any other ideas?'

Brian started to pace the island as he applied his massive intelligence to the problem. He came to a sudden halt. 'I know! We could use your mirror shades to flash a signal to passing planes!'

Pete just pointed up at the empty skies. (Secretly, he was relieved. He didn't like the idea of taking his shades off. What was the point of being rescued if you didn't look cool?)

Brian went back to pacing, Pete went back to sunbathing, and the sharks just went on circling.

★ ★ ★

As the last of the water in the tank gurgled down the plughole, Tammy was feeling hopeful. Not only had help arrived in the form of the little suckerfish, but also, after that dip in the water, she would be able to skip her monthly bath for once.

Out in the lagoon the suckerfish swam to the side of the glass wall and clicked a button. Its voice came over an intercom: 'Hello, friends. My name is Watson. I wonder if I might be of assistance?'

'You could tell us what's going on,' said Curly. 'Have you seen the prisoners in the other holding tank?'

The suckerfish nodded. 'It seems that a secret group has had this lagoon constructed by a team of crab construction workers.'

'But why?'

'My only guess is that the sharks live on a diet of kelp,' said the suckerfish, 'but they aren't all happy about this. Some of them long for the old days . . .'

'Back when they used to eat other animals?' said Tammy.

'That's barbaric!' exclaimed Curly. 'Eating animals is wrong,' he added, remembering his history lessons from school. 'As my old teacher said, "It isn't polite to try to eat something you could discuss the weather with."'

'Nevertheless,' said Watson. 'I believe these other sea creatures have been lied to. They have been brought here so that a secret group of sharks can hunt them in these private grounds.'

'We have to get out,' said Tammy. 'We have to free the other prisoners and tell people what's going on.'

The suckerfish nodded. '*Splendid.* There's a button on this control panel. I think it opens an airlock into the lagoon. You can swim up to the rubber raft out here.'

'Then what?' asked Tammy nervously.

'Don't worry,' said the suckerfish, its sucker-pad quivering. 'I'll think of something.'

Peregrine was back on the choccy bickies to ease his nerves. For the first time in twenty years, he could remember what happened that awful day when his ship sank.

'At first those sharks weren't going to do anything,' he told Lola. 'But there was a creepy little suckerfish with them. It kept whispering to the lead shark, things like, "You can't beat a bit of pig for supper," and "Pork is the other white meat." He wouldn't stop talking, and finally the sharks started listening to him.

'I said, "Pipe down, you little sucker!" That's when he said he wanted his name to be the last thing in my mind. He told me it had a special meaning.'

With trembling trotter, Peregrine wrote the letters down on a notebook page. Lola wasn't surprised at the name:

W
A
T
S
O
N

Then Peregrine wrote next to the letters:

W Who's
A
T The
S Sucker
O
N Now?

'That's what he told me his name stood for: "Who's the sucker now?"'

'What about the A and the O?' asked Lola. 'Didn't he like vowels?'

'I would have asked,' huffed Peregrine, 'only I was busy trying not to be eaten.'

'And you're sure the phone message was the same suckerfish?'

Peregrine nodded grimly. 'I'd recognize that voice anywhere. If the rescue helicopter hadn't pulled me out of the sea just in time, it would have been the last thing in the world I ever heard. That suckerfish is pure evil.' He looked at the words CHUM Luxury Breaks on Lola's computer. 'Even the company name is a creepy little joke. It doesn't mean *chum* as in *friends* — it means chum as in the bits of meat and blood people used to throw to sharks years ago.' Peregrine sighed. 'Whatever's going on at Shark Island, he'll be behind it.'

'But what can we do?' Lola bit her lip. 'We've lost radio contact with the team.'

Peregrine shook his head. 'We really must get some better radios.'

Then the Wing Commander got to his trotters and sighed. 'There's nothing else for it.' He heard himself saying something he thought he'd never utter. 'Hold the fort, Lola. I'm going back to Shark Island!'

CHAPTER 8:

Pig Hunt

Curly was horrified to have to swim one more time, but with Tammy's help he made it from the airlock up to the rubber raft. Tammy pointed back to the other holding tank where Headstrong and all the other fish could be seen, their faces pressed against the glass wall. Some of them were waving their fins and tails urgently at the two pigs. Tammy waved back.

'Can you let them out, as well?' she asked the suckerfish.

'I'm afraid not,' said Watson.

Curly wasn't paying attention to any of

this. He was watching three enormous pale shapes moving through the dark waters of the lagoon behind the suckerfish. As they got closer, three huge fins broke the surface.

'Behind you!' he shouted. 'Great white sharks!'

'That is most kind.' The old suckerfish smiled calmly. 'However, I am well aware of what is behind me.'

Suddenly Tammy understood. 'You're part of this, aren't you?' she said to Watson. 'A group of evil sharks has set up this hunting ground, and you work for them. I'm right, aren't I?'

Watson's sucker-pad quivered. 'You're wrong! This place *is* a shark hunting ground, but I work for nobody.' He smiled proudly. 'I suppose it doesn't matter if I tell you now.

This whole place was my idea. I planned it, designed it, had the crabs build it. I wrote the job ad to attract our victims. And now today, we are finally open for business! These great whites are our first clients. They are Fang, Frenzy and – perhaps the most deadly predator in the ocean – Mrs Susan Prendergast. Our opening day is going to be quite *splendid*!'

Curly was confused. 'What's all this got to do with Neil Headstrong and his mission?'

'The hammerhead came up with that entire scheme in his own pea-sized brain,' answered Watson. 'Naturally, I didn't want some thicky shark wandering about inland and ruining my plans.

That's why I got myself a job with his team. I tried to convince him that his idea was pointless. Usually I can persuade sharks to do anything, but Headstrong lives up to his name. Once an idea has lodged in that misshapen head of his . . . So, in order to stop him ruining everything, I had to go to Plan B – instructing one of the crabs to snip his water supply.'

'But he might have died!' exclaimed Curly.

'I don't think he cares,' said Tammy. She pointed at the main holding tank full of fish. 'So you lied to all of them too?'

'Not at all,' Watson explained patiently. 'I offered them an exciting job opportunity with plenty of exercise. And is that not true? Is it *not* exciting to be chased by a shark?'

Tammy snorted. 'So this was all just about making money then?'

The suckerfish looked hurt. 'Good

gracious, no!' He pointed a fin at the huge sharks swimming laps below him. 'Feast your eyes on them! They are perfection! The shark is a *perfect* eating machine, ideally designed to hunt its food – NOT to shovel disgusting, smelly kelp burgers down its pie-hole. They will hunt and eat any creature in the sea . . . except clown fish, that is – apparently, they taste funny. Sharks are, in a word . . . *splendid.*'

'So you persuaded a bunch of weak-willed sharks to try to turn the clock back to the Bad Old Days of eating meat?' spat Tammy.

'Have you ever tasted a Burstin' Bucket o' Kelp?' snapped Watson. 'The box is tastier than the contents!' He took a gulp of water, as if to rinse his mouth out. 'And I'm afraid, Miss Snuffles, that I cannot agree with you. We are recapturing the glories of the GOOD Old Days. The thrill of the chase,

the scent of blood, and then, of course . . .', his sucker-pad jiggled excitedly, '. . . the *kill*!'

A giant head rose from the water. Its eyes were as black as night. 'Did someone say KILL?' snarled Fang.

A second head appeared. Its teeth were as sharp as knives. 'We're starving,' growled Frenzy. 'Let's get started!'

A third head popped up. The lipstick around its giant mouth was as red as a cherry. 'I just love what you've done with this place!' twittered Susan.

Watson quickly explained to the great whites that they could choose their victim for the hunt now. He listed all of the different fish in the holding tank, mentioning each one's speed and probable tastiness.

'Octopus looks tasty,' said Fang.

'Eel looks good,' said Frenzy.

Watson then waved a fin at the pigs on the raft. 'Or . . . if you'd prefer to hunt something a little more exotic, we have two land mammals.'

The great whites eyed the two pigs on the raft, and Curly now knew what a baked bean must feel like as it sits on the toast with all its mates.

Fang scrunched up his nose and said, 'I'm not sure I'll like foreign food.'

Frenzy said, 'Won't the meat be fatty?'

But Mrs Susan Prendergast's voice

dropped to a terrifying, low rumble: 'Today we're hunting pig.'

'As you say, Susan,' said Fang hurriedly.

'Pig it is!' agreed Frenzy, nodding frantically.

'How delightful!' Mrs Susan Prendergast simpered, going back to her normal voice.

Watson smiled in approval of the choice. '*Splendid.*'

Back on the desert island, Pete's snout twitched. 'Can you smell bacon?'

'That'll be my skin,' moaned Brian. 'I burn in the sun. When I was at school, the other piglets used to call me Sunday Roast.'

'But you covered yourself with Factor Thirty sunblock just five minutes ago.'

'I know,' agreed Brian sadly. 'I can't find the Factor Sixty.'

After a couple more laps around the island, Brian stopped again when his foot struck something half-buried in the sand.

'A bottle!' he cried out. 'We can put a message for help in it!'

Pete wasn't impressed. 'It'd take days to reach someone.' He pulled the bottle out of the sand. 'Look, there's a message already in here.'

He shook out the bit of paper and read: 'TWO EXTRA PINTS OF MILK AND A RASPBERRY YOGHURT, PLEASE.' Pete sighed. 'Oh, dear.'

'What?'

'There's a date here too – Tuesday the eighth.'

'That was only yesterday!' said Brian.

Pete threw the note aside. 'Tuesday the eighth *twenty-three years ago!*'

'Oh . . . That yoghurt's probably gone off by now then.'

Brian returned to his anxious laps as the hungry sharks went round and round.

★ ★ ★

Shark Island's first ever pig hunt was about to begin.

'What if we just stay on this raft?' Tammy asked.

Watson smiled icily. 'My guests would probably get a little cross. I imagine they'd just tip the raft over and eat you within seconds.'

Tammy stepped forward (though not far enough to fall off). 'This isn't fair! How can we outswim a shark?'

'You don't *have* to outswim a shark,' answered Watson, pointing at Curly. 'You only have to outswim *him*.'

'Hold on,' Tammy said. 'You needn't involve Curly in this. He's just a piglet. There's no meat on him anyway. He can't even swim! Where's the sport in that? If you're looking for a challenge, *I'm* the pig you want.'

'You can't do that —' Curly began, but Tammy hushed him quickly, whispering, 'Use your head!'

The suckerfish consulted with the great whites underwater and then, to Tammy's surprise, he popped up and said, 'Very well. The piglet can stay here. As for you — we shall give you five minutes' head start from the moment you enter the water. Don't waste time looking for an escape — the walls are too high and the Exit Stream to the sea only opens from the other side. Do you have any questions?'

'Yeah,' snarled Tammy. 'Will you stop pointing that sucker-pad on top of your head in my direction? It's disgusting.'

If Watson was angry, he didn't show it. 'You needn't worry your little land-based head about that, Miss Snuffles,' he said. 'My pad will most certainly not be on view . . . I shall be accompanying the lovely Mrs

Prendergast on this hunt. And now, game
on! Or perhaps that should
be . . . *gammon*!'

With this, he swam
down and attached
his sucker-pad to a
spot below the biggest
shark's jaws.

Tammy took one
last look at Curly and
then stepped off the raft.

The hunt was on!

Pete and Brian were no closer to finding a
way off their little island.

But, after a few dozen more laps, Brian
noticed a couple of pieces of driftwood
washing up on the shore.

'I know!' he cried. 'We can use these pieces
of wood, along with your oxygen tank, to
build a raft! We'll tie them with palm leaves!'

He saw the look on Pete's face. 'Don't worry – I've read all about this in *An Illustrated History of Raft Design and Construction*, volumes one to five.'

Pete wasn't sure, but he shinned up the palm tree anyway. It swayed worryingly under his piggy weight. Minutes later the pigs had strapped together the driftwood and the oxygen tank to make a raft.

'I've read all about sharks,' said Brian. 'They mostly rely on sensing vibrations in the water to catch their prey. So all we have to do ...'

'... is not vibrate very much?' Pete guessed.

'Erm, yes,' said Brian, sounding slightly less confident. 'If we drift gently towards the plane, there's every chance the sharks won't even know the raft is anything but another bit of driftwood.'

Pete thought it over. 'Can we just give it a test run first?'

When the shark in the closest 'lane' had swum by, the pigs stood at the water's edge and eased the raft slowly into the sea.

'Well, it floats,' said Brian approvingly.

Seconds passed.

'This might just work,' murmured Pete.

A huge grey head loomed out of the water and crashed down on to the raft, smashing it apart. The two pigs hopped backwards on to dry land just in time.

'Then again . . .' said Pete.

Tammy was a strong swimmer, but knowing that three great whites would soon be after her didn't do much for her front-crawl technique.

She stayed close to the edge of the

lagoon. She could never outswim her pursuers, so she was looking for a place to hide.

A distant cry reached her ears. It was Curly: 'Tammy! They're coming!'

Panic jolted through her. She swam towards a darker patch of water up ahead. She reached it and saw it was a patch of tall seaweed, almost up to the water's surface.

An idea hit her. Treading water, she dipped into her top pocket and pulled out a ballpoint pen. She used her teeth to pull the cap off the bottom and pull out the pen's inside bits. She popped the empty plastic tube into her mouth, then dropped below the surface. Her body was now hidden by the seaweed, and with her head tilted upwards, she could use the pen case as a snorkel.

From here, she could peek out of the seaweed and look around. She was in a shallow section of the lagoon. The seaweed clump she was hiding in was the last in a line of three clumps. The water around her seemed eerily empty.

But then something appeared out of the blue. Fang! He was taking his time, trying to use his shark senses to locate his prey. Tammy held her breath and kept as still as possible.

The shark swam a slow zig-zag, coming closer and closer. Tammy felt sure it was heading right for her, but it glided past, just metres away.

Tammy breathed a silent sigh of relief. This feeling lasted for about five seconds, until Fang swept back into view. He had completed a wide loop and was now back at the first clump of seaweed. He paused, and then attacked, ripping into it. Shredded weeds and dust from the bottom flew everywhere in a slow-motion underwater

explosion. If Tammy had been in *that* clump of weeds, she'd be diced ham now.

Next, Fang swam the short distance to the second clump of seaweed. Tammy watched in horror as he started to attack it.

It didn't take a genius like Brian to work out what was going to happen after that. Fang would turn his attention to the seaweed she was hiding in.

CHAPTER 9:

Swimming with Sharks

If they didn't get off this little desert island surrounded by sharks soon, Pete was going to go bonkers. The only way to mark time was by watching Brian slowly turn a deeper and deeper shade of red.

'If you get any more sunburned, you're going to start smoking,' Pete said. 'But then maybe someone will spot the plume of smoke?'

Brian paid no attention. He was scribbling some calculations on a scrap of paper. At last, he looked up with triumph on his face.

'I've got it!' he said.

'Is that "Got it!" like the last few *Got its*? Cos I'm not sure they were really *Got its*, technically speaking.' Pete didn't want to hurt his friend's feelings, but he didn't want to get gobbled up in a feeding frenzy either. 'Sorry, Brian. Your ideas are brilliant. They're just not always *practical*.'

Bri pushed his glasses up his snout defiantly. 'This time I've *really* got it. One of us is going to FLY off this island!'

Worrying that the medic must be suffering from sunstroke, Pete asked gently, 'How's that then, Bri?'

Brian pointed to the palm tree. 'I got the idea from *The Illustrated Pop-Up Encyclopaedia of Medieval Weapons*,' he explained. 'We'll turn that tree into the biggest catapult ever!'

Pete shook his head. 'Sounds crazy,' he said. 'Sounds dangerous.' He adjusted his mirror shades. 'Sounds like my kind of fun! Let's *do* it!'

Tammy swam as if her life depended on it. Which, in fact, it *did*. She didn't dare look behind for a telltale fin racing towards her.

As she headed further into the open water in the middle of the lagoon, her arms and legs started to feel like lead, but there was something poking out of the water ahead of her. It looked like a coral reef, but turned out to be just a plastic model. Like the small stone castle and the statue of a deep-sea diver she'd spotted on the lagoon bottom, it was just there to make the chase a little more interesting.

Tammy swam around the 'reef', looking for good hiding spots. There were none. Allowing herself a moment to catch her breath, she held on to the fake reef with one trotter and scanned the surface. With her other she unzipped a pocket in her flightsuit and pulled out the last can of Cherry Slurpo-Pop.

'According to the advert, Slurpo-Pop makes everything better,' she thought grimly. 'Let's hope that's true.'

But when she popped the ring-pull, some of the fizzy drink gushed out into the water. As Tammy saw the spilt pop forming a crimson cloud in the water, she knew exactly what it looked like – blood! She

remembered Brian saying that sharks could detect even a few drops of blood in the water from hundreds of metres away. Well, Slurpo-Pop didn't *smell* like blood in the water but it certainly *looked* like it. If one of the sharks spotted it . . .

'Uh-oh,' Tammy murmured.

Back on the raft, Curly hadn't a clue what was happening out in the lagoon, but he was pretty sure it wasn't good. He was sure of something else – whatever they had promised, when the sharks had got Tammy, it would be his turn next.

The trainee's mind was galloping. *What should I do?* The last thing Tammy had said was, 'Use your head'. What did she mean by *that*?

He glanced back at Holding Tank 1. How long before those poor sea creatures were released to be hunted down as food?

He wondered what the hammerhead Neil Headstrong must make of this. What thoughts were going through his oddly shaped head?

Hold on, thought Curly. *Maybe I shouldn't use MY head . . . maybe I should use SOMEONE ELSE'S head.* If only he could get Headstrong out of that holding tank!

Curly remembered where Watson had opened the control panel for the smaller tank. It was probably the same for the bigger one.

There was just one problem — it would mean going back in the water. Just the thought made all the bristles on the back of his neck stand to attention.

He looked down into the water and tried to face his many fears. Water up the nose? *Easy — just hold your snout.* Seawater stinging your eyes? *No problem — stinging eyes never killed anyone.* He was starting to feel more confident. So what else was he afraid of? Drowning? Being chomped by a vicious predator of the deep? OK, these two points *were* a bit trickier.

'Think of Tammy!' he told himself. 'You're a PiP now! And for PiPs, the only thing to fear is fear itself. So just count to three and jump in.'

Curly counted aloud, 'One . . . two . . .'

The water looked dark and cold.

'Two and a half . . .'

Who knew if one of the sharks was still nearby?

'Two and three-quarters . . .'

He looked out and saw a fin in the distance. Was it heading for Tammy?

'THREE!'

Curly jumped.

His immediate instinct was to flail about wildly, but for once he overcame this. He even opened his eyes and turned towards the holding tank. Slowly, with one trotter still holding his snout, he swam towards the control panel.

All of the sea creatures in the tank watched him carefully through the glass wall. Curly pulled off the panel cover to reveal . . . an alphabet keypad! He had to key in a password! But *what*? Without air, his heart was thudding like a speed-metal drumbeat. He would have to push up to the surface soon.

What password would Watson pick? he asked himself. Quickly he punched in the word SHARK. It did nothing. Curly tried again with GREAT WHITE, then REMORA. Nothing and nothing. The same was true for HUNT. Curly's lungs felt as if they might pop soon. He couldn't hold on much longer.

Suddenly something loomed out of the murky water. It was Mrs Susan Prendergast!

The great white was zooming towards him,
mouth open, a hellish pit framed by double
rows of dagger-like teeth, top and bottom.
From the shark's underside, Watson was
eyeing Curly hungrily too. The suckerfish
was grinning eagerly and mouthing
something. Curly couldn't hear it, but he
knew what the suckerfish was saying, and it
gave him an idea.

He just had time to punch the letters in – SPLENDID – then hit the button. It worked! The exit door started to open.

But now the great white was almost upon him.

'It's dinnertime!' bubbled the suckerfish gleefully.

'No, it's HAMMER TIME!' gargled Headstrong, shooting out of the holding tank and straight into Mrs Susan Prendergast. The great white was bigger and stronger, but Headstrong caught her by surprise. He knocked Susan off course, just enough for Curly to squirm away. The next thing the pig knew, a protective cloud of squid ink surrounded him, and a pair of eels were pulling him to safety.

As he reached the surface, he sucked in enormous lungfuls of fresh air. How had he never before noticed how brilliantly sweet air was?

'Where's Headstrong?' he gasped.

'Gone to help your friend,' answered one of the eels.

'And where's Susan?'

'Gone to stop him, the only way she knows.'

'How's that?' asked Curly.

'With her teeth!'

As Tammy trod water and waited for the sharks to arrive, an idea tickled at her brain.

She'd heard that in the Bad Old Days just the sight of blood in the water could drive a shark into a feeding frenzy. Maybe, just maybe, Slurpo-Pop *could* make everything better.

It was worth a try – Tammy took one last swig, burped, then emptied the can into the water. A dark red cloud blossomed around her.

Moments later she spotted the first fin.

Almost immediately, a second appeared from the opposite direction. Both were moving fast. Tammy waved one arm in front of her to churn up the water and spread the cherry pop as far as possible.

Fang and Frenzy were almost here. If they'd been thinking straight, they might have wondered why this 'blood' smelled exactly like artificial fruit flavours, but just the sight of it had driven out all other thoughts. They went blood-crazy. Both sharks shot forward into the spreading cloud, and smashed right into each other.

As Tammy rolled back into the water, the sharks thrashed around and snapped wildly at each other, driven mad by the idea of blood.

Tammy didn't waste any time patting herself on the back. It would take the sharks only seconds to calm down and remember she was in the water with them.

She searched quickly for something to fight with.

All she could find as a weapon was the rope still coiled over one shoulder. She knew that it would be as effective against the great whites as a pea-shooter against an armoured car, but she still bunched it up ready to throw.

The sharks lunged faster than she'd expected, but what happened next was completely unexpected. As she hurled the rope at the oncoming great whites, another shark – a hammerhead! – caught it. Headstrong!

He grabbed one end of the rope in his teeth, splashed down, then swam away . . . leaving Fang and Frenzy right in front of Tammy!

'Do you want to say any last words?' Fang smirked.

'Just this . . .' said Tammy, looking down

at the end of the rope in her trotters. 'BYE-
EEE!'

With Headstrong pulling the other end of
the rope at high speed, it soon completely
unwound, and when this happened the
PiPs mechanic shot off. Water slapped into
her face as Headstrong gained speed and
dragged her through the lagoon.

But the great whites weren't about to let
dinner get away. When Tammy looked back
behind her, she could see two fins giving

chase – and then a third, even bigger one not far behind – the dreaded Mrs Susan Prendergast.

'Go faster!' Tammy yelled to Headstrong as she bounced across the water.

The hammerhead pulled her through a narrow channel carved into the rock. Tammy knew this must be the way out of the hidden lagoon, back to the open seas. Behind her, the great whites seemed to be getting closer, close enough to see that Fang's big pointy teeth needed a good cleaning.

The walls on either side became higher. Tammy glanced ahead – they seemed to be zooming towards a rock wall, but then she realized that the waterway carried on *underneath* the rock.

'The *exit* must be near,' she told herself, preparing to hold her breath. But then a dreadful thought struck her. Hadn't Watson said that the underwater exit only opened from the OUTSIDE?

So that meant they were blasting towards a dead end!

CHAPTER 10:

REALLY Extreme Watersports

'Now!' shouted Pete.

Brian cut the rope and the palm tree *SPROINGED* upright. Pete flew off in the direction of the SkyHog jets.

The PiPs captain loved all extreme sports, but flying had a special place in his heart – even planeless flying. Nothing could beat being a heavily built pig defying gravity.

He soared upwards, with barely a glance for the circling

sharks below. As he reached the highest
point of his arc, he faced the island ahead of
him. From this height, he could actually see
the channel that led back to the sea. What's
more he could see a hammerhead shark
zooming down it, towing an object so large
and pink it could only be one thing – a pig!
And close behind them was a line of three
great white sharks! Pete realized that they
were heading towards the hidden doorway
he had seen earlier – which was currently
closed!

He looked back down, to see that he was
hurtling towards the water. It wasn't quite

as near to the SkyHogs as Brian had figured – probably because Pete had lied about his weight when the medic was doing the calculations. It didn't matter anyway – it was time for a change of plan.

As he hit the water, he didn't start swimming to the planes. Instead he dived deeper and deeper, down towards the spot where he'd seen the secret doorway. He knew he also didn't have long before one of the tiger sharks came for him.

Finally he reached the right patch of rock face and pulled back the starfish to reveal a button. All he had to do was push it, just as the pilot fish had done.

Moments later, the hidden entrance to Shark Island slid open in a spray of bubbles.

That should do it, thought Pete. *Now I'm going –*

Before he could finish his thought, a hammerhead shark shot out of the exit.

Seconds later a pink pig-shaped blur went by.

Tammy! thought Pete.

Right behind her came one of the great whites.

Time to get out of here, Pete decided. Extreme sports fan or not, even he knew that swimming with renegade meat-eating great whites was not a sensible leisure activity. He frog-kicked his legs to reach the surface.

Suddenly the second great white appeared from the hidden exit and its snout shot right between Pete's open knees. If it had been just centimetres lower, there might have been enough clearance for the dorsal fin. As it was, the fin slammed painfully into Pete's belly. 'OOF!' Instinctively, he gripped on to it, and the shark swam on. Now all Pete had to do was hold on tight and ride the Shark Express.

From the desert island, Brian had watched in horror as his captain landed short of the planes.

'I don't understand,' the medic muttered. 'I *triple*-checked those calculations!'

He waited anxiously for Pete to reappear but there was no sign of the PiPs captain. The two tiger sharks furthest from the island started towards where Pete had landed.

The seconds stretched. Was Pete *ever* going to resurface? If not, what could Brian do? All of his brilliant ideas so far had failed. Feeling helpless, he watched the patterns of the sharks still circling the desert island — clockwise, anticlockwise, some slower, some faster, each in his own lane . . . The SkyHogs sat not too far beyond the furthest of the

sharks. And that's when one last idea popped into Brian's head. Was it brilliant? *Yes.* Was it practical? *No.* Would it work? *Almost certainly not.* But with Pete nowhere to be seen, Brian had to try.

He started counting the sharks' laps, just waiting for the perfect moment – that one instant when all the circling sharks lined up. It only occurred every seven minutes, but it was coming up . . . NOW! Brian raced into the water and leapt. His left trotter landed on the closest shark, right in front of its dorsal fin. Kicking off before the shark could snap at him, Brian sprang forward again to the next shark, which was swimming in the

opposite direction. Without stopping, Brian leappigged from this shark to the next, then from that one to the shark beyond.

This was the last shark, but Brian jumped one more time. He landed on the pilot fish. Unlike the sharks, the little fish was not built to take the weight of a full-sized pig. When he woke up, he was going to have the worst headache ever. But Brian didn't have time to celebrate. He started swimming as fast as he could towards the nearest SkyHog.

An Olympic-standard piglete might have made it, but Brian was more of a *quick-paddle-then-sit-by-the-pool-and-read* type of swimmer. He knew there wasn't much chance of him reaching the plane before the sharks got to him, but he didn't stop trying. He swam by a couple of pieces of floating driftwood, the remains of their earlier raft. Knowing that the tiger sharks must be closing in on him from behind, he grabbed one piece. At least he wouldn't go down without a fight.

Suddenly he saw a different fin break the surface a few metres ahead of him. Long hours reading *The Penguin Spotters' Guide to Shark Fins* meant that Brian, of all the PiPs, could identify shark species by their fin alone. This was a hammerhead, and it was swimming away fast. Then something *else* rose up out of the water, right underneath him. It swept Brian out of the water at high speed. He glanced down to see Tammy between his legs!

'Sorry, Bri!' Tammy cried in mid-air.

'Not at all,' he called out, remembering his manners.

As the pigs crashed back down, Tammy's trotters landed on one bit of the driftwood. Still gripping the rope, Tammy stood on the driftwood as it skimmed across the water.

She took off like a water-skier, with Brian sitting across her shoulders!

They were heading away from the jets now and out to open sea. From his position on Tammy's shoulders, Brian could see a large tanker on the horizon. It was steaming towards them. Although he wobbled alarmingly, Brian risked a quick look back at the tiger sharks chasing them. They didn't look happy. Nor did the two great whites also barrelling towards them. One of them appeared to have something on its back. Brian blinked away the sea spray in his eyes – if he didn't know better, he'd swear it was Peter Porker!

It was! Pete had swung his legs around the fin so he was facing forward like some crazed, overweight jockey. When Frenzy became aware of his passenger, he began to live up to his name. First he dived down in a spiral of bubbles. Pete held his breath and grabbed on tightly. Next Frenzy leapt up out of the water. Still Pete held on. In fact, he was starting to enjoy this! When the shark jumped out of the water again, Pete raised one trotter and waved it around in classic cowboy fashion, 'YeeHA!'

He promptly fell off.

He thought Frenzy would loop back for him, but the great white swam off after Tammy and Brian, towards the huge tanker that was coming ever closer. However, even with Frenzy gone, Pete still wasn't exactly safe – not when two of the tiger sharks were zipping his way.

Suddenly he heard the sound of a jet engine firing up. SkyHog 1! But who was in the cockpit? With Tammy and Brian busy waterskiing, there could be only one answer – Curly McHoglet! The two eels had towed the trainee off the island and, because all of the sharks were busy chasing other members of the PiPs, the eels had been able to reach SkyHog 1 unharmed. Moments later the jet was zooming across the surface of the water. When it picked up enough speed, it rose into the air. The two water-skis folded back into the undercarriage.

The sight of his jet back in the sky filled Pete's heart with hope, but not for long. Those two tiger sharks were getting closer and closer. It wasn't a question of IF he'd get eaten, or even of WHEN. Now it was just a question of WHO got to him first.

Suddenly the most fearsome great white of them all smashed her way greedily between the squabbling tiger sharks.

'PIG!' bellowed Mrs Susan Prendergast.

But then the air was filled with a deafening SkyHog roar. A shadow passed overhead and a rope ladder slapped Pete in the face. He grabbed it just in time and was wrenched out of the water.

'Ham's off the menu today!' he called.

But Susan wouldn't give up her second pig of the day so easily. She leapt at Pete. Her immense jaws just missed his legs, but they snapped shut on the lower rungs of the rope ladder and gripped them like a vice.

The plane's engine sputtered. It wasn't designed to carry something this heavy. Unable to go any higher, it flew along with pig and shark dangling just above the water's surface.

Pete's arms ached as he clung to the rope ladder, but he had good reason not to let go – lots of reasons if you were counting all of Susan's teeth.

The plane turned now in the direction of the water-skiers, who were still zipping towards the big tanker. Pete tried to shout: 'Not that way! You'll never get enough altitude!'

But the roar of the engine drowned his words. He looked down and saw the great white inching up the rope ladder, using her teeth!

'I'll get you, pig!' she snarled.

Pete glanced ahead at the approaching ship. A familiar bulky figure stood on the prow – it was Peregrine! The PiPs commander looked his old self. He waved a signal and a troop of shark fins appeared from behind the tanker. Peregrine had come with reinforcements!

But they were too late to help Tammy and Brian. The hammerhead towing them was slowing down at last. He swerved to avoid the tanker and the two water-skiers were whipped into the air. Seizing the moment, Fang and Frenzy put on a final burst of speed, and leapt out of the water like two sea-to-air missiles with teeth.

But SkyHog 1 was on the spot too. It dipped suddenly under the weight of its load and the bottom half of the ladder – where

Mrs Susan Prendergast dangled – slammed straight into the two airborne great whites. WHACK! The impact knocked all three predators sideways, right on to the deck of the ship, while Tammy and Brian splashed down into the water. Pete saw that they were in no danger now – the sharks that had arrived with Peregrine were busy arresting the tiger sharks.

'Pull up!' Pete yelled.

With the extra weight gone, Curly pulled the plane up steeply. The rope ladder just missed the ship but Pete got a good view of the deck.

The tanker had been bringing food supplies to Shark Island. The three sharks had landed in a massive container of kelp.

'Hope you're still peckish!' Pete shouted.

CHAPTER 11:

Never Give a Sucker
an Even Break!

Down on the sea floor, someone waited.

Watson's plans were in tatters, most of
the evil sharks under arrest. Now the cursed
PiPs and their kelp-loving shark friends were
looking for *him*. They had begun swimming
out in ever-wider circles. The wretched pigs
went with them, riding on the sharks' backs.

The only one left behind was the oldest
pig – the fat one called Peregrine. He had
sailed to Shark Island and convinced the
authorities that they had to help his team.
Now he sat alone in a boat, with just

one young blue shark as a guard. Watson couldn't shake the feeling that this pig looked slightly familiar.

'We can get up now, Flat Stanley,' he said.

The camouflaged angel shark peeled itself from the sandy bottom, and Watson detached himself from the bigger fish.

He was a slow swimmer, but the suckerfish reached the blue shark without being seen. He attached his sucker-pad delicately to the shark's underside, then whispered, 'Pssst! What's all the fuss about?'

'We're looking for a suckerfish called Watson,' replied the blue shark to the suckerfish called Watson. (OK, he wasn't the brightest, even for a shark.) 'Have you seen him?'

'No,' said Watson, adding, 'So who's in the boat?'

'Pig.'

'Really? You know what they say about

pigs, don't you . . . scrumptious eating!
Absolutely *splendid*.'

'I hadn't heard,' grunted the blue shark.

Watson went on in his quiet, persuasive
way. 'Here's a funny idea. You could always
just knock him in and have a nibble. Who'd
know? They'd think he just fell in and
couldn't swim.'

The blue shark was confused, and Watson
didn't give him time to think. 'I mean, look
at him sitting there, all high and mighty –
not to mention, fat and juicy, with no fur
to get caught in your throat. Go on, just
a quick bite. I guarantee, once you've had
meat you'll never go back to kelp . . .'

'I don't think so,' said the shark
uncertainly, but suddenly there was a
SPLASH! Peregrine had been leaning over
the side of the boat to ask something. He'd
leaned too far and tumbled in.

The other unfortunate thing was that

Peregrine had cut himself shaving that morning. There was only the tiniest bit of dried blood, but its smell activated an ancient part of the shark's predator brain.

'Smell it!' cried Watson. 'That's better than kelp, eh? YES! Then get it! Rip it to shreds! EAT! EAT THE MEAT!'

With the scent of blood in its nose and Watson's insistent voice in its ear, the blue shark could control itself no longer. He flicked his tail, opened his mouth and . . .

'YUCK! That's terrible!' said the blue shark.

His teeth had no more than grazed Peregrine's arm before he pulled away in disgust. As he did so, the shark seemed to come to his senses.

'I'm sorry, sir,' he said to Peregrine. 'I don't know what came over me.'

'I do, son,' said Peregrine, treading water. 'Luckily, I got my tube of *Fletcher's*

Finest Anti-Shark Gel back from Brian. It *does* work, you know!' He reached out and peeled the suckerfish off the shark's underside.

'Get your mitts off me, you filthy mammal!' shrieked Watson.

Ignoring these complaints, Peregrine used the suckerfish's own sucker-pad to stick him to the hull of the little boat.

He grinned. He had waited twenty years to say these words:

'Who's the sucker *now*?'

EPILOGUE:

A Clean Start

'Here, Tammy,' said Pete the next day at PiPs HQ. 'I've got you a crate of Slurpo-Pop.'

Tammy wrinkled her snout. 'Thanks, but I've decided Slurpo-Pop is yucky!' She held up a bright orange can. 'I only drink Orange Bubble-GuzzleAde now. It's deliciously refreshing!' She chugged the can and belched. 'I would offer you one, but I've only got twelve cans left.'

Just then Lola burst into the common room holding a letter. 'I've won a prize from *Pig Puzzle Weekly!*' she announced. 'It's a weekend break for two on Shark Island! Would anyone like to come?'

Peregrine folded down his copy of the *Swine Times*. 'It says here that half the lagoon is going to be a holiday resort – Neil Headstrong is opening the Hammer Time Hotel there. The other half will be a kelp factory. In fact, our old friend Watson will be working there as part of his punishment. That's something I'd love to see.' He beamed. 'So yes, I'd be delighted to accompany you on the trip, Lola.'

'Great,' said Lola glumly.

'Hey, anyone know where Brian is?' asked Tammy between fizzy-pop burps.

'On the firing range,' said Pete. 'After yesterday's mission, he's got a new idea for a pig-poo catapult. I wish he'd work on something to de-frizz my hair. All that saltwater has ruined my style.'

Suddenly a gigantic brown ball splatted

against the window. SPLUDGE!

'He's still ironing out the details,' said Pete.

'Good thing it hit the *closed* window,' huffed Peregrine.

Two seconds later, another ball of pig poo shot through the *open* window. It hit the room's electric fan and exploded everywhere.

Curly jumped up. 'That's OK,' he cried. 'We can go for a swim to clean off. Right?'

Since he'd got over his fear of
water, swimming had become Curly's
favourite activity.

'That's all good and well,' said
Peregrine darkly. 'But I'm afraid
someone's going to have to clean up
this mess!'

'Don't be afraid, Commander,' said
Pete, heading out the door with the
others. 'The only thing to fear is fear
itself!'

READ MORE OiNKCREDiBLY FUNNY ADVENTURES OF THE

Crossword

 **Across→**

2. Tammy hides from the sharks behind this.

4. _____ Luxury Breaks.

6. An athletic pig!

8. They eat a lot of this on Shark Island.

10. Another name for a sucker fish.

11. Neil _____Strong.

Down ↓

1. What Curly fears the most.

2. Tammy's favourite drink.

3. The answer to Lola's crossword clue.

5. Watson's chilling catchphrase.

7. Pete's real middle name.

9. There's a secret one on Shark Island.

★Turn to page 148 for the answers.

Word Scramble

Unscramble these words:

1. **GIVNID**

2. **RAHDEMMAHE**

3. **SLIDAN**

4. **HETTE**

5. **FWODIDROT**

6. **KARSH**

7. **MONMAG**

8. **SMISION**

9. **RGAET-WETHI**

10. **LAMP REET**

★ Turn to page 148 for the answers.

Wordsearch

Find the words opposite hidden in this grid.
(Look carefully – some may be
backwards or diagonal!)

F	N	F	J	A	V	X	C	T	A	D	T
H	I	I	A	P	A	R	A	D	I	S	E
Z	M	N	C	G	Z	V	T	V	N	I	M
P	N	D	S	O	J	N	L	Y	O	S	L
J	B	C	I	R	M	D	E	V	C	F	E
M	E	O	F	N	A	M	H	F	A	O	H
M	R	I	D	B	G	F	A	A	B	W	R
D	P	P	R	P	I	H	T	N	P	X	Y
V	Q	Q	G	G	J	O	Y	G	D	X	G
H	W	A	Y	M	M	A	T	F	K	E	C
A	S	U	C	K	E	R	F	I	S	H	R

★ Turn to page 148 for the answers.

BACON SUCKERFISH

RAFT PARADISE

HELMET FIN

FANG DINGHY

COMMANDER TAMMY

Answers

Crossword

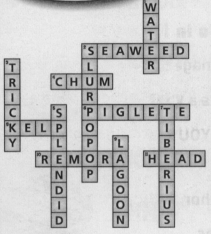

Wordsearch

```
F N F J A V X C T A D T
H I I A P A R A D I S E
Z M N C G Z V T V N I M
P N D S O J N L Y O S L
J B C I R M D E V C F E
M E O F N A M H F A O H
M R I D B G F A A B W R
D P P R P I H T N P X Y
V Q Q G G J O Y G D X G
H W A Y M M A T F K E C
A S U C K E R F I S H R
```

Word Scramble

1. DIVING
2. HAMMERHEAD
3. ISLAND
4. TEETH
5. DRIFTWOOD
6. SHARK
7. GAMMON
8. MISSION
9. GREAT-WHITE
10. PALM TREE

It all started with a Scarecrow

Puffin is well over sixty years old.
Sounds ancient, doesn't it? But Puffin has never been
so lively. We're always on the lookout for the next big
idea, which is how it began all those years ago.

Penguin Books was a big idea from the mind of
a man called Allen Lane, who in 1935 invented
the quality paperback and changed the world.
**And from great Penguins, great Puffins grew,
changing the face of children's books forever.**

The first four Puffin Picture Books were hatched in 1940 and the
first Puffin story book featured a man with broomstick arms called
Worzel Gummidge. In 1967 Kaye Webb, Puffin Editor, started the
Puffin Club, promising to **'make children into readers'**.
She kept that promise and over 200,000 children became
devoted Puffineers through their quarterly instalments of
Puffin Post, which is now back for a new generation.

Many years from now, we hope you'll look back and
remember Puffin with a smile. **No matter what your age
or what you're into, there's a Puffin for everyone.**
The possibilities are endless, but one thing is for sure:
whether it's a picture book or a paperback, a sticker book
or a hardback, **if it's got that little Puffin
on it – it's bound to be good.**